To Sam,

Hope these stories
Make you smile!

Best wishes,

THE SOUTH OVERLOOK OAKS

John Reardon

Illustrated by
Chris Youngbluth

Seven Locks Press
P.O. Box 25689
Santa Ana, CA 92799
(800) 354-5348

Individual sales: This book is available through most bookstores or can be ordered directly from Seven Locks Press at the address above.

Quantity Sales: Special discounts are available on quantity purchases by corporations, associations and others. For details, contact the "Special Sales Department" at the publisher's address above.

Cover and Interior Design by Kira Fulks www.kirafulks.com
Cover Illustrations by Chris Youngbluth

Printed in the United States of America

Library of Congress Cataloging-in-Publication Data is available from the publisher

ISBN: 1-931643-91-1

Dedication

To my wife, Leslie,
and my daughters, Sophie and Adele,
with love

Contents

INTRODUCTION

My name is Silver Leaf Oak. I am one of the South Overlook Oaks.

If there is one thing I have learned while standing in the same place for nearly thirty years, it is to be a good listener. In this book are true stories I learned by simply listening to other trees, animals and People.

You see, we Oak trees spend most of our lives listening. Sure, we have our own language, known as Swaying and Rustling. We talk to one another on a regular basis. You may hear us, especially on a windy day; our leaves rustle when we talk and our branches sway when we laugh.

Since we are stuck in one location, we communicate by passing messages from one Oak to the next. This often causes confusion, because messages get changed as they pass from tree to tree. In fact, just last week, a message that began as "The Blue Jays are coming to eat the raspberries" ended as "The blueberries are coming to eat the Rabbits".

Incredible!

As you can see, communication among Oaks is not so easy. That is why listening is one of my favorite pastimes.

So, I am here to tell you a few stories I have heard and seen among the plants, animals and People who live here on South Overlook

Drive. I have translated these stories from their original Antpatch, Birdsong, Catcall, Dogbark, Peoplespeak, and yes, even Squirrelchatter.

Chapter One

South Overlook Drive

South Overlook Drive is a gently curving street, lined with beautiful Oak trees. There are twenty houses on the street, and no two houses look the same. They are a collection of Brick Colonial and American Clapboard style. They were built in the late 1930s, with thick bricks and solid wood planking. The roofs are made of genuine tar shingles or Vermont Slate.

Every afternoon, the dozens of children who live here come out to play, and the street fills with their laughter. They play in the yards and driveways, in front porches and back patios. They hide-and-seek, skip and bike along the curb, and climb up the smaller Oaks.

I have learned a lot from the children who live on this street. I love hearing little Emma Kyle giggle when she rocks back and forth on the tree-swing that hangs from my branches. I especially look forward to Eliza Schmidt's songs. She turned five just last Summer, and when she sings at bedtime, her voice carries through the open bedroom window and travels to my branches in the soft August night.

Like the People in their homes, the South Overlook Oaks are also a family. We Oaks share the same soil, we bask in the same summer sun, and we huddle under the same blanket of winter snow.

Yes, we are a family. Old Rag Oak, to my left, and Jiminy Oak to my right, they are like uncles to me—larger and wiser in many ways.

We Oaks are comfortable here on South Overlook Drive. We stretch and grow our limbs and branches high, high above the homes. Our canopies create a wide shade across the street. On summer days at noon, children can ride their bikes along the street without ever leaving the shade of the South Overlook Oaks.

Some Oaks say this is the best place to be an Oak in the whole world. As far as I can tell, from my height of thirty feet,—they are right. This *is* the best place in the world!

CHAPTER 2

JUNIPER TELLS A STORY

"Have you heard how the Ladybug and the Firefly became friends?" asked Juniper, the young tree planted some twenty years ago. Juniper lives at the corner of the Wilsons' house, just across the street from where I stand, in front of the Dutch Colonial house now owned by the Reardons.

Juniper's high-pitched voice woke me up early one morning last Summer. I could see that the young saplings and azaleas were straining to hear the story.

"Well, have you ever seen a Ladybug and Firefly fight?"

"No!" all the young plants agreed. "No, never!"

"That's right! That's because Ladybugs and Fireflies are friends." Juniper told this story every year, but I never grew tired of hearing it.

"It was not always this way, my young friends. Ladybugs and Fireflies never played together. Until one day, in this very front yard, a Ladybug was flying along in the late summer afternoon."

The young plants were listening attentively, leaning toward Juniper to hear his tale.

"Ladybug was flying along, as usual, when suddenly a stiff breeze blew from the

West. A cold front with a rainstorm blew in, and *Poof!* The wind carried Ladybug all the way up to the top of Majestic Oak over there." Juniper pointed a bough toward Majestic Oak.

"Wow, all the way up to the top!" The younger saplings exclaimed, clearly impressed.

"Well, as you know, Ladybugs live in the grass and Lower Reaches; they never go beyond the mid-branch level. Certainly, no Ladybug would ever dare go to the Upper Reaches, where Crows and Robins make their nests. The Crows and Robins would gladly eat the Ladybugs. Those little Ladybugs would be bird bacon before you know it!"

The saplings laughed, repeating "Bird bacon! Bird bacon!" Finally, their laughter died down and Juniper resumed his tale.

"Well, once the storm blew Ladybug high up, she was too scared to come down. She sat nervously, hiding from the Crows and Robins, clinging to a leaf at the top of Majestic Oak.

"Soon it began to get dark and Firefly wanted to go home too. He blinked his light to find one of his brothers or sisters, when *Poof!* Another gust of wind blew him up into the Upper Reaches of Majestic Oak. He landed on the same leaf where Ladybug sat, and quickly scrambled to find cover so the raindrops would not shatter his delicate lantern.

"By now, the sun had set, and black storm clouds filled the night sky. Ladybug knew her parents would be worried but she could not see well enough in the dark to get home. She would be stuck on the leaf until dawn—if she survived the night at all.

"It was dark and Firefly clung beneath the same leaf as the rain continued to fall hard on Majestic Oak.

"Ladybug, you're lucky. If only I could fly in the rain like you, with your hard shell," said Firefly. *"I could go now and light my way home."*

"Oh, Firefly, you're the one who's lucky.

I can see well enough in the daytime. But at night, I am too blind to make my way home in the dark. Surely, a light is more helpful than a hard shell," said Ladybug.

"Not in this rain, Ladybug," said Firefly. "Believe me, your shell is like an umbrella. Tonight I have seen the raindrops and even hail bounce right off your hard shell, while I hide here under this leaf, which is much too thin to protect me from the storm all night."

"Well," said Ladybug "I have an idea!"

"Yes?" asked Firefly.

"What if you grab hold of my feet, and I will spread my shell above you," Ladybug said. "Then, you could guide both of us home, using your light, while my hard shell will be your umbrella!"

"Brilliant!" said Firefly.

"And so, working together, Ladybug and Firefly were able to fly down from the

Upper Reaches of Majestic Oak. What a sight they made! Firefly, lighting the way, clutching Ladybug's little black legs like an umbrella handle, while raindrops bounced off her hard shell. The two fluttered, blinking with delight, down to their homes in the hedgerow.

"Ever since then, Ladybugs and Fireflies have been best friends!" Juniper explained.

The saplings clapped their twigs, the azaleas shook their blooms, and the shoots swayed in a chorus of approval. Everyone loves a good story.

CHAPTER 3

A FRIENDSHIP GROWS

Juniper was always good for a tale, but the other Oaks are just as interesting. Scarlet Oak can predict the weather with remarkable precision. And Majestic Oak knows a million jokes, like what is a cat's favorite color? *Purr*-ple. Things like that. The South Overlook Oaks are special, each in its own way.

But it was with Old Rag Oak,—who stood to my left,—that I had developed a deep friendship over the years.

Old Rag Oak got his name because an old black costume was nailed to his trunk one Halloween night, many years ago. It must have been part of a witch or bat costume, meant to scare Trick-or-Treaters as they came up the walkway to the Jones' house. But now, there it was, a tattered cloth, the size of a large handkerchief. It had grown up with Old Rag Oak and was suspended by a rusty nail high above the ground.

We stayed up late on many nights, Old Rag Oak and I. We would Rustle-and-Sway and he would tell me stories about his younger, happy days.

Sometimes, we stayed up all night and waited for dawn to rise. I remember those occasions,—the dark sky slowly grew from black to grey and the first morning light would appear in soft shades of pink and blue. The birth of a new day!

I always admired how tall Old Rag Oak was. I was one of the younger Oaks—although not the youngest—and my generation of Oaks had only grown about thirty feet high. Not near the forty feet of some trees along South Overlook Drive, including Old Rag Oak himself. Certainly, not near the fifty feet that Morgan Oak reached in the Reardons' backyard. Now that was tall! We could easily see Morgan Oak from the front yard, even with the Reardons' house standing between us.

As the seasons changed from Spring to mid-Summer, I noticed that Old Rag Oak was beginning to lean toward me. I liked to think it was to hear me better, but that was not really why. He was tipping slightly more each day.

Late one night, after the hottest part of summer had passed, it finally rained. The thunderstorm announced its approach with a symphony of wind, building into loud thunder and falling hail.

After a tumultuous downpour, all turned quiet, and the sky turned coal black. Suddenly, it started to rain again. This time, it rained, and rained, beating down, like a drum roll— loud and pounding. Big puddles spilled into the street, and overflowed the storm drains. My bark was soaked and it dampened my inner mantle. My taproot in the ground was "tapped out" full of water. It seemed as if it would rain forever.

Old Rag and I were happy that night. The rain made us feel silly as young saplings. We laughed and sang and played—flinging droplets at each other. I called him "Whippersnapper," and he laughed. We smacked our branches together and rustled our leaves with delight.

The rain had come. We loved it!

CHAPTER 4

GROWING UP AND GROWING OLD

By morning, the storm was over. Mist hung over the Upper Reaches of Old Rag Oak, Sail Ship Oak, Majestic Oak and Jiminy Oak. Shafts of light reached the younger trees below and formed bright circles of light on the ground. Overnight, the lawn had turned lush green and some moss had matted-down around my base.

I looked up and noticed that Old Rag had lost a few branches during the storm, and —he was leaning even closer to me!

I realized then, for the very first time, that Old Rag Oak was dying I thought about his life, and how amazing it was that this soaring tree was once a small acorn, no bigger than an average June bug.

All Oaks begin as acorns, you know, but most end up as food for Squirrels or are cut down long before they have a chance to develop.

Old Rag Oak must be sixty or seventy years old by now. Of course, until an Oak tree dies, no one really knows its age. Oak trees grow outward from the centers, adding one layer of growth to the trunk each year. The number of layers, or rings, found in a cross-section of the tree, tells how many years the tree lived.

'Yes,' I thought, 'when Old Rag Oak dies, at the end we will count the rings.'

I thought some more about Old Rag Oak's difficulties. It would not be long now—perhaps a few more weeks, before he would fall over. If he was lucky, maybe he could stand up for another year—that is, if the Jones' would not call the Chip-Choppers and have him taken down first.

CHAPTER 5

THE PLAN

I felt sure that if Old Rag Oak could stand up straight, then Mr. and Mrs. Jones would not call the Chip-Choppers to cut him down. The Jones' love trees too much for that to happen.

So, the next evening, when the kids had gone home for supper and story time—and all turned quiet, I spoke to Old Rag Oak about an idea I had.

"Hi there, Old Rag. Hmmm, excuse me?!" I called out.

"Well, hello, Silver Leaf. How are you?" He said politely.

"That was quite a storm last night," I said.

"That was indeed a good thunder bumper, but I have seen storms, let me tell you!"

I interrupted before he could begin the storm stories he so liked to tell.

"Old Rag, excuse me, but I would like to ask you for permission."

"Yes, well, you may certainly ask me anything."

"Well," I hesitated, searching for the right words, "it seems to me that you have been leaning a tad bit . . . just a touch my way . . ."

"Oh, I have not noticed any change." He replied calmly.

'He had noticed, I am sure!' I thought to myself, *'How could he not notice that he was practically tipping over?!'*

I continued, "I thought that if you would permit me, I just might have a way to remedy the . . . uhhh, situation."

"Are you suggesting that I have a problem of some kind!?" He huffed.

This was not going so well! So, I tried again.

"My idea is this", I said, "Now that my taproot is full from last night's rain, I will be able to grow quickly. I could grow your way— into that sunny spot, just below your third branch, and push you up straight with my forked branch,—If you would permit me, that is."

He frowned for a while, thinking. Then he looked and, as if for the first time, he noticed my forked branch.   His expression changed. Now he was intrigued.

"Why, I see . . . " he paused.   "And how long do you think it would take before that branch reaches to push against my main trunk?"

"Well, it could be as long as three full moons," I speculated.

Several minutes passed, and then he said thoughtfully, "Young Silver Leaf, you have my permission to grow toward that sunny spot. But with one condition."

"Yes, Sir?"

"When you get over here, try to push me to the other side, just a little bit. I would not want to fall on the Reardon's house or land on you."

Exactly right, I thought to myself, *that is my hope, too.* But all I said was, "Of course. It's a deal."

"Agreed then," was all he said about it.

For the next few weeks, Old Rag Oak parted his branches and created a sunny spot for me to grow into. I grew as fast as I could.

Each time the Chip-Choppers drove by and eyed Old Rag Oak hungrily, I held my breath, hoping they would pass by without an incident.

I was so relieved when they would turn at the end of the street, and drive off, out of sight.

CHAPTER 6

SWINGING ALONG

One of the nice things about being me is having a tree-swing hang from my large left branch. The swing is made of strong hemp rope and a plank of honey-colored, solid Ash wood. The rope loops around my upper branch and descends about fifteen feet down.

The grass beneath the tree swing has disappeared long ago. Now there is an oval patch of dirt where the ground has been pounded down over the years.

The tree swing is the center of amusement on South Overlook Drive. The children stop often to visit me and I get to hear many good stories.

One recent Summer day, Sophie and Adele Reardon took turns swinging, when their Mother came out to join them. She pushed them hard, giving them underdog pushes and spinners, as well.

After a while, they took a break.

Mrs. Reardon spread a blue blanket on the grass. She opened a large wicker basket and gave the girls a colorful lunch: green apples, small bunches of purple grapes, and wedges of red watermelon. The assortment of small sandwiches looked yummy, and the girls devoured them hungrily.

When the meal was over, Mrs. Reardon said, "Now, how about a story?"

The girls nodded sleepily.

"Hmmmm . . . who has a story to tell?" asked Mrs. Reardon.

"You go first Mom!" they called out together.

So, I drooped my branches down to hear Mrs. Reardon tell her story.

CHAPTER 7

INDIAN SUMMER

"Well, girls" Mrs. Reardon began, "You know that before our ancestors arrived here, another group of people lived under these big trees."

"You mean the Indians?" asked Sophie.

"Yes, dear. The Native Americans. But not just any Native Americans. Here in Virginia, you see, lived a tribe of Native Americans known as the Powhatan."

"Poe-hat-in" the girls repeated, sounding it out.

"Yes, and the Powhatan were very kind to one another." Mrs. Reardon continued, "They lived in big wooden houses, called a longhouse, where three or four families lived together."

"Cool!" said Adele, "You mean, it would be like if the Wallers, the Schmidts, the Wilsons and our family all lived in one big house! That would be so cool!"

"Yes." Said Mrs. Reardon.

She continued, "The Powhatan were friendly people, and rarely fought with other tribes. They lived here, in the woods,—back then it was all forest, you know, there were no cities at all."

"Wow!" Sophie knew that it must have looked very different back then.

"The Powhatan people depended upon Nature for everything: food, shelter, and clothes." said Mrs. Reardon. "They did not have stores where they could buy things; they had to make everything from what they found in Nature."

"That would be hard!" said Adele. Sophie nodded her head in agreement.

"Yes, it would be hard." Mrs. Reardon agreed. "But Nature provided everything they needed. For example, they would hunt deer with their bow and arrows. The deer provided them with food and the fur was used to make coats to keep them warm. The antlers made good fishing hooks, and the deer's tendon was used for fishing line and string of their bows."

"They used everything?" said Sophie.

"That is right, Honey. They did not waste anything. They were very resourceful and made use of everything."

"Maybe they built a longhouse right here beneath this tree!" Sophie imagined aloud, and the girls crawled under the blanket, pretending it was a longhouse.

I smiled and thought of the time before these houses were here,—when longhouses dotted the forest floor and other children played here. Who knows, maybe those children had a tree swing, too!

CHAPTER 8

INTERLUDE

All in all, there are twenty Oaks on South Overlook Drive. For years, the tallest was Majestic Oak. But a few years ago, Sail Ship Oak shot a branch skyward, that just surpassed the uppermost twigs of Majestic Oak. Still, in terms of overall size, Majestic Oak is the grandest of the grand.

Majestic Oak is so massive that he barely sways in winds that shake younger trees to the mantle. He stands hefty and strong, with multiple offshoots springing from the main trunk. Even the offshoots have their own offshoots, and all these branches, branchlets, twigs and leaves are suspended in the sky, revolving around his enormous trunk, like a large carousel.

This afternoon, the wind blew hard. I could see Majestic Oak's ruffled bunches of green leaves, furling and unfurling the green and white undersides in succession, like a hundred pompoms cheering at a football game.

Later in the evening, Barn Owl came to rest in the branch hole of Scarlet Oak. Scarlet Oak was nearly fifty feet tall, with fine reddish coloring around the base of her trunk, where red clay had been wrapped into the roots. There was a branch hole halfway up her trunk, where an old branch had fallen off and left a small indentation. Barn Owl often rested there.

Tonight, I could hear Barn Owl hooting to himself about the Field Mice in the farmer's acreage a half mile or so away. Barn Owl continued hooting, going on and on about the previous night's rain and how hard it was to hunt in a storm like that.

I, on the other hand, was content to have the rain. It helped me stretch my forked branch toward Old Rag Oak. In that sense, I felt like I was running a race against time.

I had no idea whether it would be tomorrow that Old Rag Oak would fall, or six months from now. I only knew that there was not a drop of rain, nor a ray of sunshine to waste in my efforts to push Old Rag Oak away from me and stand him upright again. I could only do my best, and hope that was enough.

CHAPTER 9

SOMETHING'S SQUIRRELY!

They say that Owls are smart, and they are. But in my mind, of course, the smartest are Oaks. Then People. Probably in that order: Oaks are smartest, People next, and maybe Owls or Foxes are in third place.

Come to think of it, Squirrels are perhaps smarter than Foxes. Let me tell you a story and you decide who is smarter, Squirrels or Foxes.

The South Overlook Squirrels are lucky: they enjoy feasting on seeds in bird feeders, and trash cans overflowing with delicacies, especially old bread and leftover corn on the cob. Their favorite food is the old-fashioned acorn. Each autumn so many acorns fall from the South Overlook Oaks that the Squirrels are never able to bury them all.

They are indeed lucky Squirrels. Here, on our Street, they are also safe from all their natural enemies, except Dogs. Still, our Dogs are either kept on leashes, or they are too fat and lazy to catch Squirrels anyway.

Well, as I said, the Squirrels on South Overlook are quite fortunate to live here—they have an abundance of food, lovely yards to roam in, and fabulous nests which they build in our towering branches. They really have it made. Or so they thought, until that one fateful winter when the Fox family arrived.

It was a cold and clear February night. The bright light of a full moon glittered on the snow. In the shadows, just under the Wilsons' front window, I saw something move! It slinked, nimble and quiet, along the hedgerow. At first glance, I thought it was a Cat. "There goes Whiskers, the Turleys' Cat", I thought.

Yes, that is exactly what I thought it was— a Cat. But suddenly, and without warning, the creature pounced on a Squirrel! It was too dark for me to see what was actually happening, but I could hear the commotion in the bushes,— then the night turned quiet.

The next day, the Wilsons were puzzled. Something had devoured the Squirrel and left the discards in the bushes by their mailbox. They could not imagine that their old Dog, Maxine, would kill a Squirrel. If only they could understand my Rustling, I would have told them it was not Maxine!

Later that week, on a dark chilly evening, I saw Mr. Reardon walk behind his house to get firewood. Ahead of him, I noticed a quick movement in the dried-up bushes behind the woodpile. The unexpected commotion made Mr. Reardon stop in his tracks. He looked around for a minute, then decided to forego the firewood, and went back inside his house.

The next day, when he returned to investigate, Mr. Reardon found a dead Squirrel lying under the tarpaulin that covered the woodpile. Only bones and black fur remained.

The news traveled fast among the Oaks, and even faster among the Squirrels. Two Squirrels gone in less than two weeks!

The Squirrels chattered back and forth all morning.

"Did you hear, did you hear!? Black Tail Squirrel went out last night to grab a snack and did not return home. His black tail was found this morning behind the Reardons' house!"

"How awful!" the Squirrels cried out

"How horrible! We must be careful!" they called, warning each other.

"The children must not leave the nests without an adult!" several Squirrel Mothers warned.

Mayor Squirrel called a curfew. No Squirrel was allowed out of the trees between sundown and sunrise! "Absolutely no one!" he thundered.

The Squirrels were worried. Although they assumed that the earlier accident of Grey Stripe Squirrel in front of the Wilsons' house was a rare dog attack, this new incident was a true cause for alarm. Black Tail—found behind a house that had no dog—well, that was too much!

Later that day an emergency Squirrel Council meeting was held in Old Rag Oak's branches.

The Mayor called the meeting to order. He invited the Squirrels to give suggestions on dealing with the problem.

"Weapons will need to be gathered for the common defense," declared Bugsy Squirrel.

Six Toes Squirrel suggested the Squirrels find a watering hose and spray the monster when they found it.

'This was probably a Cat,' he speculated, 'and Cats really hate water'. He made spraying noises with his cheeks. "*Pshhhhah! Pshhhhah!*" The younger Squirrels laughed loudly and made "*Pshhhhah! Pshhhhah!*" noises for several minutes.

The older Squirrels remained serious. They knew that a Cat might kill a young Squirrel, but that a Cat would not kill a mature, heavy Squirrel. This could not have been done by a Cat, and certainly not by a Dog.

The Council agreed to send an ambassador to visit their neighbors, the Raccoons, who lived in the storm drain at the intersection of South Overlook Drive and Cameron Mills Road. The Raccoons would occasionally come down to pick through the trash,—perhaps, they would have information that would help.

Then, too, a family of Opossums lived

in the brambles behind the Jones' house, not far from the Reardons' woodpile. The Opossums, like the Raccoons, were friendly neighbors and they would be sure to help if they could.

Two Squirrels, Punched Ears and Chatterbox, were appointed to represent the Squirrel Council. They were instructed to visit with the Raccoons and the Opossums to learn all they could to help track the killer of their dear friends, Grey Stripe and Black Tail.

It was getting late in the evening and the young Squirrels were getting hungry. Suddenly, a noise below caught their attention. They froze in place and glanced down, expecting trouble, only to see Mr. Jones throw a pizza box in the trash can!

The meeting was over immediately. The youngsters scurried to the trash for a cold pizza snack.

CHAPTER 10

HOW TO TRICK A FOX

When Chatterbox and Punched Ears returned the next day from their visit with the Opossums and the Raccoons, they reported the news: A Fox family had moved into the neighborhood!

While no one was certain that a Fox had harmed Grey Stripe or Black Tail, the presence of a Fox den in the neighborhood was alarming.

The Mayor called an emergency meeting in Old Rag Oak's Upper Reaches

When everyone sat down, The Mayor cleared his throat a few times, and with a deep and grave voice, he called the meeting to order.

"My fellow citizens," he said, "We have identified those who have harmed our dear friends Grey Stripe and Black Tail. Now, we must draw a plan to stop future attacks." He looked around, satisfied with his observation.

The crowd nodded in agreement. Their Honorable Mayor was very wise—that's why he was the Mayor, after all.

"Any suggestions?" The Mayor called out to the crowd, hoping someone would know how to tackle this worrisome situation. He, for once, could not think of a specific plan.

Six Toes suggested that the Squirrels set a trap. Six Toes was clever,—they all agreed on that. They turned to him with great anticipation and listened as he laid out a plan.

They all huddled and whispered for awhile. Finally, the Mayor stood up and announced, "It is agreed, then. We will try Six Toes' idea." He paused, then added, "Let's hope it works!"

Before dusk, the Mayor and Six Toes placed Black Tail's fur in the latticework under the Reardon's front porch. The tip of their old friend's tail laid in the snow, as bait.

Then they waited for the sun to set. In the faint light of a crescent moon the Squirrels would put their plan into action!

That night, when a wispy ring of ice had passed idly across the moon, I saw Six Toes, the stately mature grey Squirrel, crawl down from his perch on Old Rag Oak and creep slowly towards the Reardons' house. He stood on the porch, scouting around for Shay-Shay, their Cat. That spoiled old menace, Shay-Shay, must have been already tucked inside her cozy house—so Six Toes walked along the railing, and with an elegant arc leapt onto the porch swing. The swing swayed lazily on its chains, making little squeaky, rusty sounds. Six Toes sat still and waited.

The swing was soft and kept him warm. It was not often he was able to enjoy such luxury. He snuggled deeper into the cushions, pushing his furry tail into the corner, feeling safe and protected.

I watched Six Toes as he drifted into a delicious snooze. Suddenly, from the corner of my eye, I saw Black Tail's fur under the porch begin to move! This was amazing! I could not believe the sight. The tail wiggled and wormed back and forth, slowly, and then it jerked. Then I heard a giggle and a familiar chuckle below the porch, and it all made sense. It was Shiney, Six Toes' youngest son. Shiney was slender enough to have climbed easily between the holes in the latticework under the porch. Out of sight and protected by the fence, he

moved the tail of the late Black Tail Squirrel. He made it look as if as if the tail was really alive.

The noise brought Six Toes into action. He began crying like a wounded squirrel, saying he had fallen from a tree. "My leg, Oh, my leg!" He pretended "I am hurt, I fell off the tree. Help me, someone! Please!"

This charade went on for a long time. Six Toes pretended to be injured while below him, Shiney swung Black Tail's fur back and forth on the ground below the porch. Six Toes continued to cry out, "My leg! My leg! I have broken it in my fall from the Oak!"

After awhile, I began to doze off. Six Toes too was getting tired, and quieted down.

Suddenly, I heard a faint sound, a slight "crunch" of a footpad in the snow.

I looked at the porch. Nothing moved.

Even the Black Tail was still. Shiney, I suspect,

had fallen asleep. He must have! His foot, wrapped in old Black Tail's fur, stuck out from under the porch.

"Shiney, wake up!" I called out to him, but Squirrels do not understand our Oak language.

I heard the noise again. Something went *Crrrk!* The sound became louder. It came from the far side of the porch.

A few moments passed. My sap began to pulse rapidly and my branches trembled with fear. I worried about Shiney. He did not move. Even Six Toes was quiet. He must have dozed off, too!

"I must do something!" I thought with panic as I saw a low, black shadow creeping along the trellis, toward Shiney! Step, *Crunch!* Pause. Step, *Crunch!* Pause. Whoever that was, he was moving very, very quietly!

I groaned and swayed, trying to wake up the pair, but to no avail!

By now the patch of icy cloud sailed away and the moon became bright. This new light gave form to the shadows, and I could see what was lurking around.

A Fox!

With his big bushy tail, sleek agile body and slinky ears, the Fox crept along the ground and held its white belly just above the snow! It made no sound as it approached Shiney. For a moment, I saw a glint of light reflect off the Fox's sharp teeth. The beast was ready to pounce!

In a flash, the Fox jumped forward and grabbed the black tail protruding from under the porch, biting it hard. Shiney yelped! He pulled back, trying to escape, but the Fox, still clenching the dead tail, dug forward with its paws, as he tried to get at the squealing Squirrel behind the lattice fence.

"Hey, Fox, up here!" Six Toes, now awake and very alert, called out to the Fox.

"Try to catch me if you can!" He egged him on, distracting the Fox so he would not harm little Shiney. Enraged by the disruption and for losing his 'meal', the Fox pulled back, dangling old Black Tail between its teeth. He shook the fur fast and furiously, then pitched it. Poor old Black Tail's fur coat flew across the yard and landed in the bushes.

Slowly and deliberately, Fox turned to the front porch. Six Toes standing in the swing mocked and taunted him to come up. The Fox launched forward but could not clear the railing, so he fell back. He circled the porch huffing, blowing and snorting when, Oh No! he suddenly found the stairs.

Quickly, the Fox jumped, leaping over the steps. In a flash, he was on the porch!

He sprang toward the swing at the opposite end of the porch, running to catch Six Toes. His big Fox eyes were intense, his nostrils wide and his mouth watering with excitement.

As he sprinted hungrily across the porch,

the unexpected happened. The ceiling fan above began to turn, and a shower of acorns fell noisily on the floor, like a hailstorm. Then I saw the Mayor, who was hiding in the rafters all along, hanging by his teeth from the ceiling fan's pull cord. As the ceiling fan swung, going around and around, the Mayor flew in circles suspended by the pull cord, seeming to fly through the air, like a trapeze artist.

The Fox, still running fast, was unable to stop. He skidded across the slippery floor now scattered with hard, round acorns. He slid uncontrollably toward Six Toes on the porch swing. Six Toes rocked back, then swung the porchswing forward with all his strength, hitting the Fox in the face with the edge of the swing.

WHAM!

It was an unforgettable collision! It is not every day that you see a speeding Fox and a wooden porch swing slam into one another! I saw the Fox's teeth fly one way, and the swing fly the other.

Embarrassed and suddenly toothless, the Fox ran off the porch, scampered across the yard, then hustled down the street,—all the way to the end of South Overlook Drive, where he turned the corner and disappeared forever.

The next day, the Squirrels celebrated their victory. They threw a party in honor of their heroes: Shiney, Six Toes, and of course their good Mayor. They presented them each with a Fox tooth tied to a red ribbon so it could be proudly worn about the neck. Every Squirrel family contributed to the festivities. There was plenty of bread crust, birdseed, and even peanut butter crackers that someone had been saving for a special occasion.

And that's how the neighborhood Fox became toothless, and life once again returned to normal on South Overlook Drive. So, if you ever ask me who is smarter, Squirrels or Foxes, you know my answer.

CHAPTER 11

ADVICE FOR THE YOUNG AT HEART

"Silver Leaf!" the voice startled me back from my daydreams. "Silver Leaf Oak, are you awake?!"

"Yes, Yes," I was quick to answer, "I was just remembering how the Fox lost his teeth."

"Those little Squirrels are clever" Old Rag Oak nodded thoughtfully.

"Listen, Son," he added with an air of authority, "as long as you're going to be growing my way,—we may as well have an understanding."

Uh-oh, an "understanding" was grown up talk for telling youngsters like me what to do.

"Okay," I said, resigning myself to a long lecture. But then again, it was a lovely afternoon and I was not going anywhere . . .

"What I mean is, you see . . ." Old Rag cleared his voice, "I have witnessed many things while standing here all these years. Things that, until now, I did not fully appreciate."

"Uh-huh," I said, Old Rag loved to tell stories and took a long time to make a point.

"But when you begin to, well, grow weak in the trunk, you get a new perspective on things.

"For example, did you know that we, Oaks, make more acorns during a dry summer than during a regular summer?"

I wanted to think for a minute before I answered him when he asked "Why do you think that is the case, Silver Leaf?!"

Again, he interrupted before I had a chance to answer.

"I will tell you why!" he exclaimed.

I wondered to myself, why he bothered to ask if he already knew the answer.

"It's because we are smart trees . . . smarter than the Locust or the Ash or the Holly, that is for sure . . ."

"Well, I think we are all as smart as we need to be." I said in defense of all trees. "Anyway, I do not like to say bad things about other trees, not even the Holly,"

"As you wish, Silver Leaf. But at my age, I must speak my mind . . ."

So he continued on about how smart Oaks are, and how observant they have been—to have learned that a dry summer is usually followed by a wet winter. And to know that a wet winter meant the ground was soft and perfect for receiving acorns. As a result, more acorns would sprout in the soggy Earth in the spring.

He said we were smart to know all that, and that more Oaks should have an appreciation of the fact that we were indeed very special trees. But he also added, with what seemed like deep sadness, that many Oaks took it all for granted.

"Yes," I thought quietly to myself, he is right. While Oaks are smart, I also think that we often take things for granted.

I was determined not to make that same mistake.

So, I started to listen to Old Rag Oak that afternoon,—really listen. He told me about his life and the older trees around him when he was young. I felt like I finally understood the life he had lived.

That evening, my forked branch finally reached Old Rag Oak!

Over the next few days, I began to slowly push him upright again. I felt pretty smart myself!

CHAPTER 12

OAKS ROCK!

The next morning, I saw Brian Waller sitting with his children on the front porch of their house, right under Red Dog Oak.

They were talking about trees and how great they are for People and the world as a whole.

"I think trees are my favorite plants," he marveled "they clean the air with their leaves like big brooms, sweeping the dirty air from the sky and replacing it with clean air for People."

Mr. Waller took a deep breath, filling his lungs with fresh air

"Why do you like trees?" he asked his children.

"Because they make syrup for pancakes," said little Maeve.

"You are right, Maeve!" smiled Mr. Waller, "that's certainly true, although syrup for pancakes comes from Maple trees,—not from Oak trees like these here.

"What else do we make from trees?"

Listening to their conversation, I began to think about it too. And then it struck me, it was almost easier to ask what was not made from trees!

People use trees for paper and pencils, furniture and fences, decks and porches, boats and toys. Trees keep People warm with fire and full with food. There are fruit trees and nut trees—all types of useful trees.

And trees decorate places, like Christmas trees and the bonsai.

With our roots, trees help to retain the soil from erosion; and we help to break up the hard clay, so that tubers and roots of plants can get a start and then grow.

Trees enrich the topsoil by adding compost layers of leaves and twigs, acorn shells and bark. The compost mixes together to supply plants with valuable nutrients on which to live.

Not only that, but everyone knows we protect them from bad weather. On hot days, we provide shade to enjoy. On stormy days, we give protection from wind and soften the rain before it hits the house and garden.

And we give to the world so much more than we take. Yes, we South Overlook Oaks are part of a proud heritage.

In addition to being good for the Earth, we trees are good company, and great storytellers. We have plenty of time to practice.

Which reminds me of a story about a young Field Mouse.

CHAPTER 13

THE BOLD FIELD MOUSE

Lately, I have noticed a little Field Mouse scampering around the front yards. He was taunting Shay-Shay, the Reardons' Cat, chasing him around. I was curious about the feisty little mouse, so I asked around. Some of the Oaks and Maples knew of him, and here is what they told me.

His name was Tim. Tim lived in the McCeneys' backyard—well, under the shed, actually. He lived with his father, Yarnball. Yarnball got his name because he looked like a frayed ball of gray yarn, all round and fuzzy.

One late night, when Old Owl was looking for a midnight snack he attacked Tim's mother. Plump little mice are one of old Owl's favorite meals and Tim's mother could not escape in time. Since then, Tim has roamed the yards without supervision.

But as everyone knows, a young Field Mouse needs care. Most importantly he needs to be taught how to protect himself: how to hide and duck, how to walk close along the walls, how to find cover in the low bushes, and to stay away from the open spaces where he could become an easy target for Birds and Cats.

So, one afternoon, when I saw Tim walking in the open yard, casually sniffing around the McCeney's flowerbed, I called to him.

"Hey, Tim, over here . . ."

He ran across the street, excited, and did not even stop to look for cars. True, no cars were around just then, but that's beside the point! He must look both ways before crossing the street!

"Oh, brother," I worried, "Young Tim the Field Mouse is too careless! It won't be long before Shay-Shay gets him, if he is not careful!"

In an instant, Tim was standing by my side.

"Hello there," I introduced myself, "I am Silver Leaf Oak, and you must be Tim." He squeaked with delight. A charming young fellow, he is, and I took an immediate liking to him.

But I continued in a low, stern voice "If you are not careful, Young Mouse, you are going to end up in Shay-Shay's fat belly!"

I expected him to show concern, to be uneasy or apprehensive. Instead, he told me a story, which made me understand why he had no fear of that Cat.

Tim, as I mentioned earlier, lives with his father behind the McCeneys' house. Now, Mrs. McCeney is French—and a fine connoisseur of French food, especially cheese and wine. Her meals are a sacred affair, and she spends countless hours preparing them.

A typical dinner at the McCeney's is never an ordinary event. It is a carefully orchestrated affair with all the rules and etiquette of the finest French restaurant. It begins with an *aperitif*, a soothing drink to whet the appetite, followed by a number of exotic and mouth-watering dishes and wine, followed by *coq au vin* or *cassoulet*, followed by more wine.

And as tradition has it, the final part of the McCeney's French meal is the cheese plate. Mrs. McCeney arranges a colorful assortment of cheese rounds on a silver platter, like an artist setting out her color palette. She places the *Camembert,* next to *Brie,* next to *Swiss,* and some *Havarti* in a circle. Then she adds a hunk of *Bleu d'Auvergne,* a bit of *La Vache Qui Rit,* some *Gouda* in the center and a slice of *Roquefort* to finish it all off.

Inevitably, with such a feast of fine food and wine, there are always leftovers in the McCeney's house, and, of course, never a shortage of cheese! Mrs. McCeney would leave the cheese plate on the kitchen counter as guests retired to the living room or lingered at the dining table after dinner.

For Tim the Field Mouse, the McCeney's house was simply Leftover Heaven!

Every evening, skinny Tim would squeeze his small body through a hole outside the McCeney's house and crawl into the kitchen wall. He would hop over the interior beams, chew his way through the insulation, force himself through a crack in the drywall and stand directly behind the stove. With a quick jump, he would arrive behind the big pots on the stove, and peek into the kitchen.

Voila! He was in!

The first time Tim entered the McCeney's kitchen he was frightened.

Mrs. McCeney stood by the stove, directly in front of him, stirring in her pots and pans.

Tim froze in place!

He stood quietly for a long, long time, watching Mrs. McCeney stir a thick white mixture of leeks and potatoes. Thank goodness, she was so absorbed in her thoughts that she did not notice him. Mrs. McCeney continued to nurture her leek soup, stirring it with a big wooden spoon, around and around, slowly and delicately, and with careful attention.

After a while, she tapped the spoon on the edge of the boiling pot and licked it. She nodded her head up and down and smacked her lips with delight.

"*Bon, Bon, Bon!*" she said, satisfied with herself. "*C'est Parfait!*"

She took another taste, then covered the pan with a heavy lid, turned down the heat and left the kitchen.

Tim peeked out of the corner and looked around. And then he saw it!

On the other side of the kitchen, on the counter by the window, sat a large, round silver tray filled with large chunks of cheese. He could smell their strong fragrance across the kitchen and his mouth began to water.

Now, as you know, when a prospector strikes gold, he shouts, "Eureka!" When a pirate finds jewels, he screams, "Treasure!" But when a Field Mouse finds a cheeseplate, he tells no one! Tim had to hide his excitement and his discovery, otherwise he would have to fight off the stampede of hungry Mice beating him to the cheese plate. Why, no doubt, such a pack of Mice would be a nuisance, an "infestation", and the McCeneys would soon call the exterminator. Then the cheese plate would disappear from the counter, perhaps forever!

Tim looked at the voluptuous *Camembert* and the hunk of seductive *Swiss*, and knew that he simply could not take that risk.

So he kept quiet. It was his secret.

Well, almost.

CHAPTER 14

CHEESE PLATE TROUBLE

The first week, when Tim went back
to the kitchen he was careful and alert. He
waited patiently on the stove, behind the warm
heavy pots. Later in the evening, after dinner
was over, the McCeneys' sat with their guests
in the living room, chatting and sipping red

wine. Mrs. McCeney returned the cheese plate to the kitchen and set it on the counter under the window. She hummed an old French song, then twirled around the kitchen before dancing her way back to her guests. Tim waited a few minutes, then quickly slipped from behind the stove, scurried across the counter, and grabbed a small piece of Gouda cheese.

He gobbled it quickly.

When he went back for more cheese, he was careful to not "break new ground," as he called it. He cautiously nibbled around the edges that were already broken off by People. He certainly did not want to leave suspicious teeth marks behind.

And so he feasted for a few weeks, returning every evening, squeezing through the narrow space behind the drainpipe, and making his way to the McCeney's kitchen where he waited in anticipation for the cheese tray to return to the counter. After Mrs. McCeney, dancing deliciously to her own tunes, would return to the living room, he would make a mad dash to the other side of the kitchen, break off a chunk of cheese and run back out.

By the third week, his daily celebration was having a noticeable impact on his waistline. He grew pudgy and round, and it was becoming more and more difficult for him to squeeze through the narrow hole behind the drainpipe.

He realized something would have to change.

If he continued to devour the McCeneys' delicious cheese, he would become too fat to squeeze into the kitchen. He had to figure out a different way.

As Tim knew, in the world of Cat-and-Mouse,—cheese is power, and with that in mind, he began to form a plan.

On his daily visits back to the kitchen, Tim began tearing off smaller bites of cheese. He would eat a few morsels and then carry the rest outside, and leave them by the Reardons' back door. He knew all too well that Cats also love cheese, and he was certain that Shay-Shay the Cat would not resist such a scrumptious treat. Shay-Shay was delighted to find chunks of cheese waiting for her by the door every morning. This was unusual, indeed, and she was curious to know how they got there.

One evening, just before she came in for the night, she noticed Tim at the back door. When he noticed her stare at him, he glanced nervously around and dashed quickly across the yard to the McCeney's old shed. Shay-Shay was surprised. "That little rascal! Who would have thought!?" She purred admiringly while chewing a mouthful of creamy cheese.

So began the unusual friendship between Shay-Shay, the fat Cat, and clever Tim the Field Mouse. Shay-Shay watched out for her little friend, she escorted him around, making sure he was safe and no one, not even Owl or Hawk could swoop away with him.

Others in the neighborhood noticed this strange friendship and wondered. A Cat helping a Mouse cross an open field in daylight

was not a common sight! Their curiosity grew when they saw Shay-Shay one day playing tag across the field with Tim. The two rolled in the grass then ran around in big circles. Shay-Shay would catch Tim in her mouth and affectionately throw him up in the air then chase him again. They played like this for hours, oblivious to others.

One evening, on his visit to the McCeney's kitchen, Tim hopped on the counter top looking for his cheese plate. To his great dismay, the tray was filled with chunks of new cheese. He hesitated for a minute, and then, against his better judgment, he bit off a round of *English Cheddar*, leaving distinctive teeth marks, and then ran out to the back yard.

Later that night, while cleaning after dinner, Mrs. McCeney noticed the strange marks on the *Cheddar.* She covered the plate and put it in the refrigerator. Early the next day she set up a mousetrap. The next evening and for many more nights, the cheese plate remained in the refrigerator before and after dinner.

Tim's happy days were over.

Soon, Shay-Shay began requesting her daily cheese treats and was becoming easily irritated and annoyed when nothing was left at her door.

Tim was in cheese plate trouble!

Then he had an idea.

A sneaky, brilliant, wonderful idea!

CHAPTER 15

SNEAKING BACK INTO THE HOUSE

The next morning Tim made up a story. He told Shay-Shay that he could not get cheese anymore because the hole behind the drainpipe had been patched and repaired. But, Tim insisted, he could get cheese if Shay-Shay would go into the house with him.

Shay-Shay listened carefully as Tim laid out his plan. The next day they set off to get inside the McCeneys' house.

Early in the morning, Tim curled in the newspaper that was wrapped in a plastic bag and laying on the McCeney's front lawn. He waited patiently for Mrs. McCeney to come out and toss the paper into the house before leaving for work.

Well, when she finally came out, Mrs. McCeney was still in her pajamas. "She is still not dressed for work?" Tim scratched his head, and then realized it was Saturday!

So there he was, scrunched in the rolled up newspaper that Mrs. McCeney now carried under her arm. He felt a BAM ! when she threw the newspaper on a stack of yesterday's mail and carried the pile with her back to the parlor. She slumped into a large leather chair and the cushions squished with a *hmmph!*

Tim could hear Mrs. McCeney sip her coffee in long shrilly slurps. She ripped envelopes, crumbled paper and threw them on the floor, murmuring things about junk and mail that he did not understand. His heart beat quickly and he wondered how long it would be before Mrs. McCeney got to the newspaper bag.

He had no time to waste.

He slid through the rolled-up newspaper, careful to not make a sound, and dropped, like a feather to the floor. He looked around quickly then scampered behind a wicker basket

He had escaped, unnoticed!

Still, he was not safe and he had to make quick decisions.

He really wanted to find the mousetrap. He thought that it would be exciting to surprise Mrs. McCeney the next time she checked the trap. He ran along the baseboards. The McCeneys' house was one big maze. "At least they don't have a pet," he thought as he jetted from room to room.

After a while, he found the kitchen. He jumped on the counter, hoping to nibble on some cheese crumbs. But the tray was not out. He wiggled his nose and sniffed the air. A faint smell of cheese filled his nostrils. He followed it all the way to the cabinet under the sink and with great effort pulled the door open. To his horror of horrors, he saw a brand new mousetrap stuffed with a big chunk of *Cheddar* cheese, the very same flavor that got him in trouble in the first place!

At the sight of the cheese, his mouth began to water, and his stomach rumbled with hunger. At first, he wanted to reach out and eat it. It took great self-restraint to hold back. He had to think clearly and fast. There was no room for mistakes this time.

He scampered up to the counter top. The green dish sponge was just what he was looking for. He carefully placed the sponge on top of the trap, covering the tripwire to keep the spring from releasing. He took another look at the cheese and with a great sigh he turned back and ran out.

Now, to complete his plan, he had to get Shay-Shay inside the house.

He scurried about the main level—the front door was closed and there was no way out. He heard Mr. McCeney upstairs, pacing the floor, talking on the phone. So he ran to the basement. It was dark and the air was musty. From the corner of his eye, he noticed a faint light coming from a little window high by the ceiling. He climbed up and sat on the windowsill, his little heart pounding with excitement. He was relieved when he pushed against the window and it opened easily.

He was out!

He found Shay-Shay stretched out by the mailbox.

"Quick!" he said. "I found a way in the house!"
She stretched lazily.

"Quick," he was irritated, "I found the cheese!"

Finally, she followed. They ran to the side of the house and squeezed through the open basement window into the McCeneys' basement.

They heard Mr. McCeney walk around in the kitchen. "We must be careful," Tim said. "Let's wait here for awhile." Shay-Shay was only happy to continue her nap on the shaggy rug.

It took awhile for Mr. McCeney to leave the house. After what seemed to be hours, Tim and Shay-Shay heard the front door slam and the sound of a car engine fade. It was a gray Saturday morning and Mrs. McCeney was asleep in the parlor, curled up in her chair having a delightful little nap.

Finally, all was quiet.

Tim and Shay-Shay looked at each other with a mischievous smile and went upstairs. Tim ran ahead and Shay-Shay followed gingerly, holding her tail up in the air, savoring each moment.

"Hurry," Tim called to her impatiently, "Now, all we need to do is find the cheese plate."

His trap was now set!

CHAPTER 16

LOST AND FOUND. . .AGAIN!

"Tim," said Shay-Shay, "this better be good cheese. If I am caught in this house I will never live to see my ninth life."

"Don't you worry," Tim assured her, "everything will be fine."

But Tim had another plan. He knew that the only way Mrs. McCeney would resume placing the cheese on the kitchen counter after dinner, was if she suspected Shay-Shay was the cheese thief.

Shay-Shay, of course, did not have a smidgen of an idea what was about to happen.

Shay-Shay was so happy to finally be inside the McCeney's home, and was naturally a curious cat, that she wanted to see every room. Tim had no choice but to take her on a tour. After she climbed and lingered on every bed, sofa and chair, and left a trail of fur and fuzz, they finally arrived in the kitchen.

"Look there," Tim whispered, "There, Shay-Shay, over there! That's where I usually find the cheese!"

He pointed to the chunk of Cheddar cheese under the kitchen sink. The green sponge was still lying on the trap, concealing the spring below.

At the sight of the cheese, Shay-Shay's green eyes grew big and wide. She slunk forward looking at it hungrily.

"Why is it covered up like that?" she asked.

"Oh, that sponge must have fallen off the counter" Tim looked away, embarrassed to look at the Cat's eyes.

Still unsuspecting, Shay-Shay smiled and licked her whiskers. She sniffed again, allowing the rich dry fragrance of *Cheddar* to penetrate her nostrils and stimulate her taste buds. In a flash, she opened her mouth and bit into it.

Whack!

The wire trap snapped up then slammed loudly against the green sponge!

Shay-Shay let out a loud *Hiss!* She jumped, arching her back. Her tail puffed into a huge porcupine ball. She was ready for the attack!

By this time, Tim was halfway down the stairs to the basement.

Mrs. McCeney woke up in a startle. Still sleepy, she ran into the kitchen to check the commotion.

"You Cat, you!" she cried with surprise at the sight of the Cat in her immaculate kitchen. "How did you get in here?!"

Stunned, Shay-Shay scrunched her back into the corner. She was not sure what to do or where to go. She looked around for Tim, but he was nowhere to be found.

Mrs. McCeney waved a wooden spoon in the air, yelling at Shay-Shay and opened the back door to let the poor Cat out. *"Shoosh!"* She snapped "And don't ever come back in this house!"

At least, Mrs. McCeney thought with relief, now I know who has been eating all my cheese!

Oh, Shay-Shay was mad. She ran out to look for Tim.

"How could you set me up like this, you little twerp." She hissed when she found him hiding under his shed. "I am your only friend! Don't you know that I could eat you up for lunch with one swoop of a bite?"

Tim knew that all too well. He really did not mean to hurt, he explained, he only wanted to confuse Mrs. McCeney so she would bring back the cheese plate.

"I wanted to give you more cheese, Shay-Shay, because you are my best friend!"

Shay-Shay could not hold back and smiled. Yes, Tim had tricked her, but now, their mission was accomplished and life could go back to normal.

Mrs. McCeney began leaving the cheese plate on the kitchen counter again after dinner. And every night Tim would sneak in, grab a few chunks, then meet Shay-Shay in the back yard and they would nibble away together.

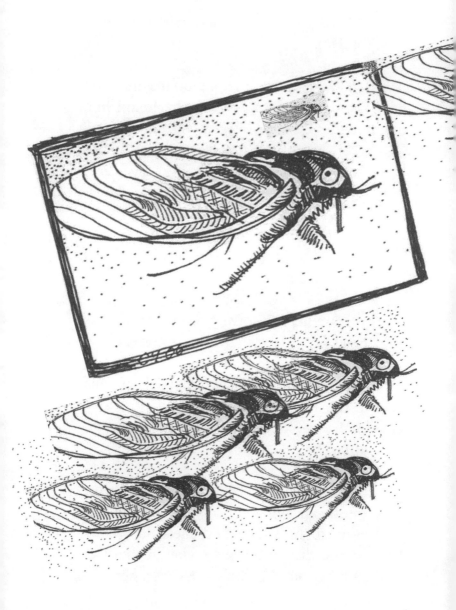

CHAPTER 17

THE 17-YEAR ITCH

As incredible as that last story may sound, let me tell you another story, maybe even more incredible.

It is a proven scientific fact that every seventeen years, the Cicadas emerge from their burrows in the ground. These noisy and not so pretty bugs awaken mysteriously one spring as if a silent signal has passed throughout the underground world. They poke little pipe holes in the ground and millions of them climb up to the surface all at once.

They lay on the grass for a few hours while their wet new wings dry and strengthen, then they fly around haphazardly, bumping into everything. I am convinced that Cicadas have the worst sense of navigation in Nature. They bump into People's foreheads and bang off parked cars. They smash into tree trunks, and collide with mailboxes. The sight of swarming Cicadas would be amusing, were it not for the fact that for two weeks millions of them dash around, buzzing, day and night. Then, as if on a silent signal, they begin to ascend the trees.

They crawl up our bark, reaching for the top branches, and there they sit. Some of us find ourselves laden down with thousands of these inch-long beasts. I myself hosted dozens during their last molting season. But, when I was twelve years old, and not so strong, they were much too heavy for my branches. It was a difficult experience to say the least! They dug into my bark, ate up my leaves, and wreaked havoc with my branches and twigs. But it was their non-stop buzzing that gave me the biggest headache. A few days later, they shed their old skin, like snakes, and left the crusty shell in my branches. Then on a signal, they marched by the thousands, out of the trees and down to the ground, where they laid their eggs in their old burrows and promptly died. It was quite a strange sight!

In another seventeen years, the next generation will emerge from the ground, and they will buzz and shrill for two weeks, lay eggs and die.

I have always wondered about those mysterious Cicadas, and one day I decided to ask Owl about them. Owl, you see, is one of the wisest creatures I have met. He knows something about everything.

I asked him why Cicadas only come out every seventeen years; he puzzled over my question for a long moment.

This time I must have baffled him!

Owl thought a little longer.

I repeated my question, "Why," I asked, "Why do all Cicadas hatch at the same time and only once in seventeen years?"

"Well," Owl finally spoke, "perhaps it is this . . ." He said thoughtfully, "Think of all the animals that eat these Cicadas. When they are here, I eat them every day. Crow, and Cat, and Opossum, and Raccoon and every Bird I know, all eat them too. Even Fox did not stay away. We all eat them, stuffing ourselves. What a feast!" he said, clicking his beak longingly.

"Owl," I said, "so what does that prove?"

"Well," he replied, "I think it proves their point."

"Their point? Huh!?" I said, even more confused than before.

"Well, you see," he explained "what I mean is this: if they came out every year, in smaller numbers, we would eat them all . . ."

"You mean . . ." I interrupted, "that by coming out all at once, they overwhelm our ability to eat them all?"

"Correct! By sheer numbers alone, they survive!" Owl concluded proudly

"Yes, Silver Leaf," he continued, "By sheer numbers they ensure their survival. Just like your acorns. The Cicadas, like all of us, are smart. Mother Nature is smart, that's for sure!"

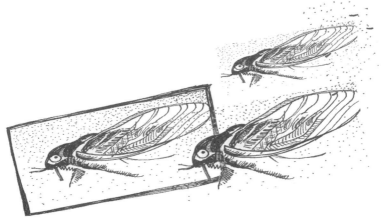

CHAPTER 18

A PERFECT LANDING

I suddenly noticed that Old Rag Oak was listening to Owl and I debate the virtues of Cicadas and Mother Nature.

"Mother Nature is very wise, indeed." Old Rag Oak added.

"You see, Silver Leaf, in Nature, nothing is wasted. Nothing. Everything is recycled: just as the rain becomes the sea, so the sea becomes the rain again. The rain helps grow an Oak. An Oak grows acorns. Acorns feed the Squirrels. Then Squirrels are food for the Foxes. And so on, my young friend."

As Old Rag Oak finished saying this, he smiled. Then he looked at me and gave a deep sigh.

"Goodbye, young tree." He said after a long minute.

Before I had a chance to ask him what he meant, I saw him sway from side to side, towards me then away, until he tipped backwards and in an instant fell over. Seventy years of life, fallen in just a few seconds.

Old Rag fell right on the Jones' car and smashed it. No one was hurt.

"Oh, we can replace the car," I heard Mrs. Jones say when she came running out of her house to see the cause of such a loud crash. "But it will take many years before we can replace that beautiful Oak tree."

The Jones children were sad. They loved their old Oak, and would miss popping the crowns off acorns and jumping in leaf piles each Fall.

The Reardons were also sad to see Old Rag Oak go, but they thanked him quietly for falling away from their house.

For the next few days, everyone in the neighborhood came by to visit. They stood around and told many stories about Old Rag Oak. Some children brought flowers and someone tied a ribbon around his trunk. One of the Turley boys used the old rag cloth as a black pirates' eye patch; standing on the fallen tree, he pretended to be a buccaneer aboard a pirate ship.

After a few days, the Joneses bought a new car. Then one day the Chip-Choppers arrived and cut up Old Rag Oak into firewood.

They made mulch from his bark for the garden and threw his leaves on the compost pile behind the Jones' house.

Some Squirrels moved their nests to my Upper Reaches, while others set up house at Jiminy Oak and Majestic Oak. And soon life went on busily as ever.

Chapter 19

From Acorns to Great Trees

Yes, everything returned to the way it was before. But I had changed. I realized too late that I missed Old Rag Oak. The extra sun I now received was no fair trade for the loss of his companionship. I felt more alone now, and all grown up. It took me a while to get over this feeling of sudden emptiness.

All that Winter, in fact, I sort of sulked and felt sorry for myself. I did not realize how much I would miss him until he was actually gone.

But by then, of course, it was too late to do anything about it. "I should have told him," I thought, "how right he was about everything. Like when he told me Oaks are smart. And Nature is never wasteful. And so many other things."

Old Rag Oak would have been proud of me, I made sure, in the years that followed.

He would have liked the way I kept a watch on the grass to make sure it got enough water through my branches to avoid drying out. And how I kept Owl company at night, when he was in-between hunting. Even the way I stretched out my canopy to cover part of the space left when he was gone. I was sure to keep my branches lofty and strong.

That next Spring, I noticed a sapling at the edge of a patch of light where my friend

Old Rag Oak had stood the Autumn before. It was not much of a sapling, but when the Summer came and went, and the mower had not run it over, I began to give it a chance. It was probably twenty leaves tall by the Fall. And thirty leaves tall by the next Spring.

There were others like it, too. From small acorns, great trees grow. Beneath Majestic Oak, three or four saplings were taking root. And over by Scarlet Oak, a Maple had made significant inroads where Scarlet had lost a branch and there was now sunlight the last year or so.

The Reardon girls, Sophie and Adele, came out and began to swing on my tree swing. I could hear their laughter as it floated up to me.

And with the wind going through my branches, I began to laugh as I swayed with the breeze.

~ THE END ~